CATCH
SOCCER'S
BEAT

STONE ARCH BOOKS
a capstone imprint

JAKE MADDOX
GRAPHIC NOVELS

Jake Maddox Graphic Novels is published by
Stone Arch Books, an imprint of Capstone.
1710 Roe Crest Drive
North Mankato, Minnesota 56003
www.capstonepub.com

Library of Congress Cataloging-in-Publication Data
is available on the Library of Congress website.

ISBN: 978-1-4965-9712-0 (hardcover)
ISBN: 978-1-4965-9922-3 (paperback)
ISBN: 978-1-4965-9757-1 (eBook PDF)

Summary: Bianca is thrilled when her parents
announce that her abuelo is coming to live with
them. Bianca and Abuelo share a love of soccer, and
she can't wait to share her love of drumming with
her grandfather too. But when Abuelo arrives, he
has his own ideas about how Bianca should practice
and play. Those ideas translate into trouble on the
field. Can Bianca find the beat in her feet before it
costs her team the tournament?

Designer: Cynthia Della-Rovere

STARTING LINEUP

BIANCA

ABUELO

TIANA

MOM

DAD

My abuelo once said to me, "Bianca, if you do something you love every day, you'll be happy every day."

Bianca! Time to go!

Well, then I'm extra happy today because I get to do *two* things I love.

Coming, Mom!

And I'll see you later!

One of the things I love is making up rhythms.

And the other . . .

. . . is feeling the beat in my feet on the soccer field!

Today's game is super important.

If we win or tie the next four games, we're in the end-of-summer tournament.

But lose even one, and we're out.

No way are we going to lose.

FWEET!

Not if I can help it, anyway!

As center midfielder, I am a link between offense and defense.

Here! Here!

I help set up plays.

Gargh!

Yes!

And move the action in the right direction.

Go! Go! Go!

I work to shut down the other team's offense . . .

Here we go.

. . . and shake it off when something goes wrong.

Get ready, Crushers!

The thing about me is, I don't just play soccer.

I hear it too.

The soft sounds.

The touches.

The passes.

For me, the sounds and tempos and rhythms are part of the game.

But I play my best when I feel the beat in my feet.

And it might seem strange.

The rhythm of the game is fast paced.

Corner kick!

Hey, awesome blast! Keep 'em coming!

But sometimes . . .

It slows wa-a-ay down.

OK, B. Make it count

And then—

The tempo speeds up again—fast!

Yes!

14

After every game, I have a special ritual.

And more than ready to play my drums!

I'll record you!

We'll get dinner going.

I think about the sounds I heard on the pitch.

And I turn those sounds into rhythms.

Are you going to play this for Abuelo later?

Sure am!

Shower first.

BZT

That rocked!

I have another ritual that's just as special as drumming.

After every game, I video chat with Abuelo—my dad's dad.

Soon, though, I'll be able to talk to Abuelo in person.

Girls, we have something to tell you.

Abuelo is coming to live with us for a while!

Really? That's awesome! But why?

He's tired of the long, cold winters where he lives now.

So he's moving here, where it's warm year-round.

MAINE

CANADA

ARIZONA

GULF

MEXICO

Until he finds his own place, he'll stay with us.

Bianca, we hoped you'd let him have your room.

Oh. Yeah . . . that makes sense, I guess.

You can have the spare bed in my room, B!

The trundle bed?

Just for the summer.

Or until Abuelo gets settled in a new place.

That was a month ago.

Tomorrow, I move my stuff into Tiana's bedroom.

I'm going to miss not having my own room . . .

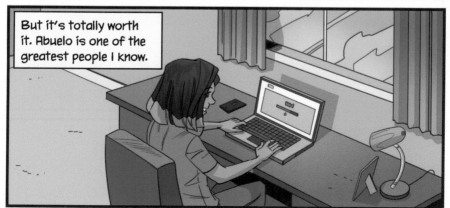

But it's totally worth it. Abuelo is one of the greatest people I know.

. . . and the rabona.

Impressive footwork by Carlos Rivera!

Riv-er-a! Riv-er-a!

His hard work paid off—big time!

When he retired, he moved to the United States with my abuela.

They had a son—my dad.

My abuela died before I was born.

I'm honored to be named after her.

MARIA BIANCA RIVERA
+
BELOVED WIFE AND MOTHER.

And I'm proud to continue the Rivera soccer tradition.

Who knows? Maybe I'll be as good as Abuelo some day!

RIVERA 7

INCOMING CALL FROM BIANCA

But for now, I'm happy to play with the Crushers.

. . . and we won on the corner kick! I can't wait for you to see our next game in person!

Me too! I'm looking forward to being closer to you and seeing you show off on the field.

Well . . . not everything went right in the game today.

I got tangled up with a defender when she ran up to steal the ball.

Ah, yes.

Next time a defender rushes you, fake to one side.

Pull the ball with you but just a little.

Then quickly pull the ball the other way.

And *vroom!* Off you go!

My teammates were right about one thing, though . . .

Sharing a room with Tiana was a little rough!

Yikes!

HAAAWWW SHOO!

HAAAWWW SHOO!

But I didn't care because . . .

There he is!

Like soccer!

I really want to show off my drum skills. But I also want Abuelo to feel at home.

And I love soccer.

So of course, I say yes!

As I always say . . .

Nice kick, Abuelo!

WHUMP!

Do something you love every day . . .

. . . and you'll be happy!

I can't wait to watch you play tomorrow.

Me too.

At the game the next day, I'm excited knowing Abuelo is in the stands.

Go get 'em, Rivera!

I'm nervous he's there too. It's the first time he's seen me play in person.

I want to play well, but . . .

What if I mess up?

FWEET!

Bianca! You with us or not?

Ah!

31

My rabona is an epic fail. And then it gets even worse.

Go! Go! Go!

No, no, no!

Yes! Yay! Woo-hoo!

BOOM!

And just like that, the Yellow Jackets are on the board.

And I come off the field.

Bianca's coming out? She hardly ever comes out!

I can't believe I messed up that badly.

Oh, Bianca.

Luckily, my teammates don't give up.

Yay! Woo-hoo! Crushers crushed it!

Final score: Cobalt Crushers 1, Yellow Jackets 1

36

Well, then let's practice it!

After my epic fail, though, I'm not sure I'm ready to try the rabona again.

What I want to do is play my drums.

Feeling the beat always helps me feel better.

But Abuelo wants to help me improve my game.

So I say yes.

OK! Let's go!

This isn't my usual postgame routine . . .

Dribble forward and plant your weak side foot next to the ball.

But it makes Abuelo happy. And I can always play my drums later.

So I give it my best shot.

Lean back and away from the ball.

Like this?

Swing your kicking leg behind the plant leg.

Hold on . . .

Abuelo makes it look easy.

I saw Abuelo early the next morning.

Ree-ea-allly early.

What are we doing here?

We're here to practice, of course!

The rabona again?

That . . . and more!

Lighter, quicker taps, Bianca! Move, move, move!

TAP TAP THUD! THUD!

Now plant your foot, lean away, swing your leg behind, and kick!

TAP TAP THUD! THUD!

SWISH!

WHUMP!

Excellent! Now do it again! And again!

After an hour of practice, I'm ready to head home, but . . .

Now let's move on to something just as good. The back heel kick!

Another new move?

41

I know Abuelo wants to help me improve.

But the more I listen to his coaching . . .

Plant your foot, then swing your leg!

TAP THUD!

The less I feel the beat in my feet.

WHIFF!

So I try to explain the problem.

It's footwork, Bianca, not something you hear!

I do better when I hear the move, Abuelo.

But I can tell he doesn't quite get it.

So I stop trying to explain. . . .

And stop trying to feel the beat in my feet.

Yes! Well done!

I focus on the motions instead.

POM!

With practice, I get better at the rabona and the back heel kick.

Wait until you see her new moves in action!

Show us tomorrow, B. Your team is going to crush the Green Hornets!

Oh, I don't know. The Hornets aren't very good. I think we can win without those moves.

But then my teammates pass along some surprising news.

The Hornets beat the Yellow Jackets!

We've gotta bring everything we have tomorrow!

Yeah! Don't wanna be bounced from the tournament!

Maybe I'll try those moves after all.

43

44

So instead, I stick with beats I know.

Here! Here!

And then I hear the sweetest sounds in soccer!

Yes!

SWISH!

The assist gives me a confidence boost.

Great pass, B!

Thanks! Great shot!

CRUSHERS
HORNETS

Next time, I'll feel the rabona rhythm! Or maybe the back heel beat!

The chance for a back heel kick comes ten minutes later. But just when I'm closing in on the beat . . .

. . . I lose it!

Halftime couldn't come quickly enough after that.

CRUSHERS	01
HORNETS	01

And when the second half starts . . .

I'm right where I deserve to be. On the bench.

The Crushers still manage to get the win—no thanks to me.

And even though I cheer, I don't feel like celebrating.

I'm sorry the back heel kick backfired, Bianca. I shouldn't have shouted while you were taking it.

No, Abuelo. I shouldn't have tried it. I wasn't feeling it. Not really.

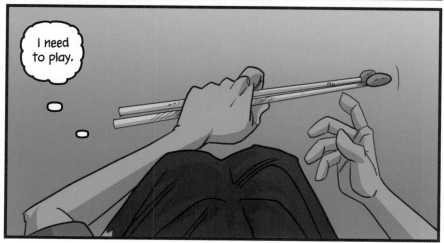

I feel the beat not just in my feet . . .

. . . but in every part of me.

It doesn't just feel great.

It feels right.

I could go on playing for hours.

But then I hear a new sound.

CLAP! CLAP! CLAP! CLAP!

CLAP! CLAP! CLAP! CLAP!

My sweet, strong, talented girl!

My sweet, strong, talented Abuelo!

I want to practice your moves, Abuelo.

But to do them right, I need to work out the rhythm. My rhythm.

I get it now.

Abuelo's kick is perfect. He figured out his rhythm long ago.

I'm still working out my rhythm. But I know I'll find it, just like he did.

My turn next!

A few days later, we have our final game. Win, and we're in the tournament. Lose . . . and we're not.

I'm sorry for how I played last game.

It's OK, B. We all have off games.

Just tell us it won't happen again! Especially against the White Lightning.

Nope. I've got my rhythm back now.

I hope.

Am I really back to my old self?

The sound and feel of that first touch unlocks something in me.

TUMP!

And suddenly, I know. . . .

I am one-hundred percent in sync.

Help!

Here! Here!

With my team . . .

. . . and with the rhythms I feel.

From that moment on, I feel the beat in my feet.

TAP TAP THUD!

I dodge defenders like they're cones.

Vroom! Thanks, Abuelo!

DODGE!

TAP TAP THUD!

My passes are on target.

WHUMP!

And when the tempo of the game stops . . .

I get it going again.

The ref calls a foul and gives the Lightning player a yellow card—a warning to be careful.

She gives us something else.

With an indirect free kick, whoever kicked couldn't send the ball right into the goal.

Someone else had to touch it first.

The moment before the kick is like a pause in the beat.

And then . . .

The beat flows over me.

WHHMP!

THUD! THUD!

BUMP! BUMP!

Every new sound adds to the rhythm.

And that rhythm drives me forward, taking me from one move . . .

. . . to the next.

I love the sound of my foot connecting with the ball.

But the next sound is even sweeter.

It's a win for us . . .

. . . and a happy day for me. I got to do both things I love.

On to the tournament!

TUMP! TUMP!

BUMP!

THWAP!

BOOM!

Tomorrow, I'll add a third thing.

I'll get to play soccer with Abuelo and his new friends!

Riv-er-a! Riv-er-a!

Which one?

VISUAL QUESTIONS

1. Abuelo says that the most important things he brought with him are his memories. What do you think he means by that? What clues in the panel below help you figure out what he's talking about?

2. Bianca's teammates aren't as excited as she is by her abuelo moving in. What does the art on pages 22–23 tell you about her teammates experiences with their own grandparents?

3. Bianca and Abuelo each have different ideas about how she should practice soccer. Flip through the story and find three examples of how they differ in their approaches. Be sure to look at both the text and art.

4. Graphic novels don't always use dialogue to tell readers what's happening on a page. How do the sound effects on this spread make the action clear? Are there other spreads in the story that use the same technique?

5. Creators of graphic novels decide what to show and not show in each panel. This is called framing. Why do you think the creators chose to show only Bianca's hands on page 37?

There are a few important things to know before taking the field in soccer. Each team starts with eleven players on the field—a goalkeeper, plus a mix of defenders, midfielders, and forwards. But what do each of those players do? Which is the right position for you? Read on to find out more.

SOCCER POSITIONS

Goalkeeper—The goalie is the last line of defense. This player is in charge of protecting the net and keeping the other team from scoring. A goalkeeper is also called a keeper or a goalie. The goalie is the only player in the game allowed to use his or her hands and arms. (Keep in mind, that only applies in the penalty box.)

Defenders—These are the players closest to the net. Their job is to help protect the goalie by blocking shots from the opposing team. They also prevent the other team's offensive players from passing, receiving, and taking shots on goal. Defenders can be fullbacks, wingbacks, and sweepers.

Midfielders—These players, also known as halfbacks, play in the middle of the field. They help connect a team's defense and offense. Midfielders see the most action during a game and do a lot of running. That is because these players can be both defensive and offensive. Some midfield positions are: center midfielder, wide midfielder, attacking midfielder, and defensive midfielder.

Forwards—The primary goal of forwards, or strikers, is scoring. This is an offensive position, and these players usually stay on the opposing team's half of the field—at the midfield line or farther. Forwards are usually the fastest players on the field and must be good at receiving passes and handling the ball. Forwards must also make sure they avoid being offside—meaning they are past the opposing team's last defender without the ball in their possession.

GLOSSARY

assist (uh-SIST)—a pass that leads to a score by a teammate

confidence (KON-fi-duhns)—to trust in a person or thing

defense (di-FENS)—a player or players who line up in the defensive zone to prevent opponents from getting open shots on goal

foul (FOUL)—an action that is against the rules

offense (aw-FENSS)—the team, or part of a team, that is in control of the ball and is trying to score

ritual (RICH-oo-uhl)—an action that is always performed in the same way

rhythm (RITH-uhm)—a pattern of beats, like in music

signature (SIG-nuh-chur)—the move for which a player is best known

tournament (TUR-nuh-muhnt)—a series of matches between several players or teams, ending in one winner

tradition (truh-DISH-uhn)—a custom, idea, or belief passed down through time

ABOUT THE AUTHOR

Stephanie Peters has been writing books for young readers for more than twenty-five years. Among her most recent titles are *Sleeping Beauty: Magic Master* and *Johnny Slimeseed*, both for Capstone's Far-Out Fairy Tale/Folk Tale series. An avid reader, workout enthusiast, and beach wanderer, Stephanie enjoys spending time with her children, Jackson and Chloe, her husband Dan, and the family's two cats and two rabbits. She lives and works in Mansfield, Massachusetts.

ABOUT THE ARTISTS

Eduardo Garcia works out of Mexico City. He has lent his illustration talents to such varied projects as the Spider-Man Family, Flash Gordon, and Speed Racer. He's currently working on a series of illustrations for an educational publisher while his wife and children look over his shoulder!

Jaymes Reed has operated the company Digital-CAPS: Comic Book Lettering since 2003. He has done lettering for many publishers, most notably Avatar Press. He's also the only letterer working with Inception Strategies, an Aboriginal-Australian publisher that develops social comics with public service messages for the Australian government. Jaymes is a 2012 and 2013 Shel Dorf Award Nominee.

READ THEM ALL!

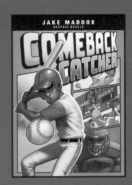

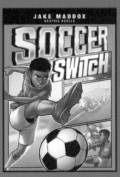